Level 2 is ideal for children who have received some reading instruction and can read short, simple sentences with help.

Special features:

Frequent repetition of main story words and phrases

Short, simple sentences

One day, Peter Rabbit was playing with Lily and Benjamin.

"What's that sound?" said Peter.

Large, clear type

The rabbits ran and ran.
"We have to hide!" said Lily.

"Look at the squirrels playing up in the trees," said Peter. "We could hide up there."

Careful match between story and pictures

Educational Consultant: Geraldine Taylor
Book Banding Consultant: Kate Ruttle

A catalogue record for this book is available from the British Library

Peter Rabbit TV series imagery and text © Frederick Warne & Co. Ltd &
Silvergate PPL Ltd, 2013
Layout and design © Frederick Warne & Co. Ltd, 2014
The 'Peter Rabbit' TV series is based on the works of Beatrix Potter.
Peter Rabbit™ & Beatrix Potter™ Frederick Warne & Co.
Frederick Warne & Co is the owner of all rights, copyrights and trademarks
in the Beatrix Potter character names and illustrations
Text adapted by Ellen Philpott

Published by Ladybird Books Ltd
80 Strand, London, WC2R 0RL
A Penguin Company

005

ISBN: 978-0-72328-091-0

Printed in China

Note to parents, carers and teachers

Read it yourself is a series of modern stories, favourite characters and traditional tales written in a simple way for children who are learning to read. The books can be read independently or as part of a guided reading session.

Each book is carefully structured to include many high-frequency words vital for first reading. The sentences on each page are supported closely by pictures to help with understanding, and to offer lively details to talk about.

The books are graded into four levels that progressively introduce wider vocabulary and longer stories as a reader's ability and confidence grows.

Ideas for use

- Begin by looking through the book and talking about the pictures. Has your child heard this story before?

- Help your child with any words he does not know, either by helping him to sound them out or supplying them yourself.

- Developing readers can be concentrating so hard on the words that they sometimes don't fully grasp the meaning of what they're reading. Answering the puzzle questions at the end of the book will help with understanding.

For more information and advice on Read it yourself and book banding, visit **www.ladybird.com/readityourself**

Book
Band
7

Treehouse Rescue

Based on the Peter Rabbit™ TV series

One day, Peter Rabbit
was playing with Lily
and Benjamin.

"What's that sound?"
said Peter.

"It's Mr Tod!" said Benjamin.

Mr Tod wanted to make
the rabbits into a pie!

"Run!" said Peter.

The rabbits ran and ran. "We have to hide!" said Lily.

"Look at the squirrels playing up in the trees," said Peter. "We could hide up there."

The rabbits called up
to Squirrel Nutkin.
"Help! We want to hide.
Could we make a
treehouse up there?"

"In our trees?" said
Squirrel Nutkin.
"You have to pass our
Squirrel Test first!"

"First you have to climb the Shaky Tree," said Squirrel Nutkin.

So Benjamin climbed the Shaky Tree.

"Hooray!" called Peter and Lily.

"Now you have to cross the Web of Terror," said Squirrel Nutkin.

So Lily crossed the Web of Terror.

"Hooray!" called Peter and Benjamin.

"Now you have to cross the Great Big Gap," said Squirrel Nutkin.

So Peter took one big jump.

Whee!

But the gap was just
too big. Poor Peter!

The squirrels pulled
him up.

"We didn't pass
the Squirrel Test,"
said Benjamin.

Just then, there was a sound. "Screech! Screech!"

"What's that sound?" said Peter.

The rabbits could see a big owl.

"Look! The owl is going after Squirrel Nutkin," said Peter. "We have to help!"

"We have to cross the Great Big Gap," said Peter. Benjamin and Peter took Nutkin and... whee!

They crossed the Great Big Gap!

"Hooray!" called
the squirrels.

"You DID pass the Squirrel
Test!" said Squirrel Nutkin.

So the rabbits did get a treehouse to hide in.

And Mr Tod did not get to make the rabbits into a pie!

How much do you remember about the story of Peter Rabbit: Treehouse Rescue? Answer these questions and find out!

- Who wants to make the rabbits into a pie?

- What does Lily have to do in the Squirrel Test?

- What does Peter have to do in the Squirrel Test?

- Who chases Squirrel Nutkin?

Look at the pictures and match them to the story words.

Peter

Benjamin

Lily

Mr Tod

Squirrel Nutkin

Read it yourself with Ladybird

Tick the books you've read!

For beginner readers who can read short, simple sentences with help.

Level 2

- Beauty and the Beast
- Chicken Licken
- Rumpelstiltskin
- Sleeping Beauty
- The Gingerbread Man
- Doris's Dragon
- Little Red Riding Hood
- Nature Trail
- Sports Day
- Pirate School
- Sly Fox and Red Hen
- The Tale of Jemima Puddle-Duck
- The Three Little Pigs
- Why Lion Roarrrs!
- The Big Race
- Town Mouse and Country Mouse
- School Bus Trip
- Topsy Tim Go to London
- The Princess and the Frog
- Treehouse Rescue

For more confident readers who can read simple stories with help.

Level 3

- You won't like this present as much as I DO!
- The Elves and the Shoemaker
- Hansel and Gretel
- Harry and the Bucketful of Dinosaurs
- Jack and the Beanstalk
- The Red Knight
- Fuji on Music Island
- Poppet Stows Away
- Rapunzel
- Aladdin
- The Jungle Book
- Roxy and the Great Escape
- Angry Birds Chuck!
- Angry Birds Bomb's Best Birthday